The Jungle

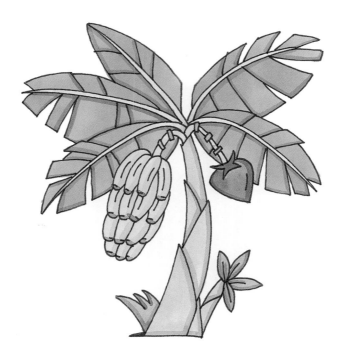

Illustrated by Kelvin Hawley

Rigby

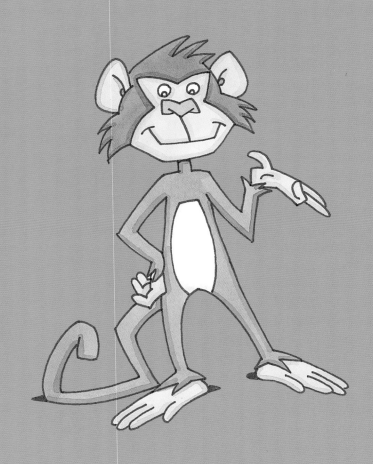

the monkey

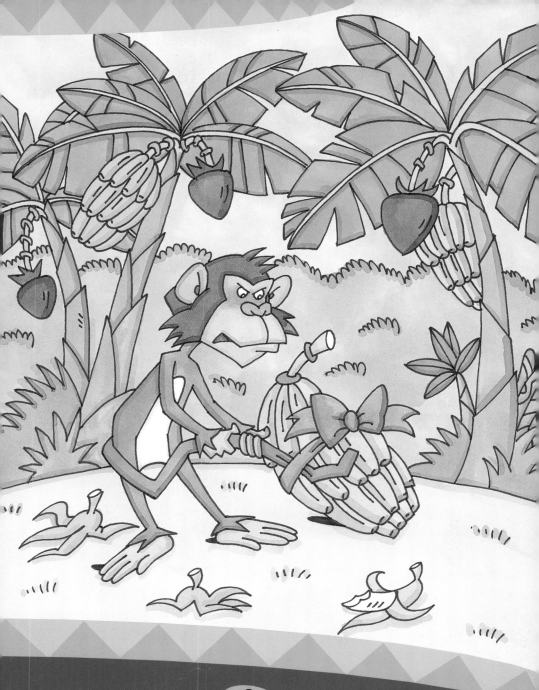

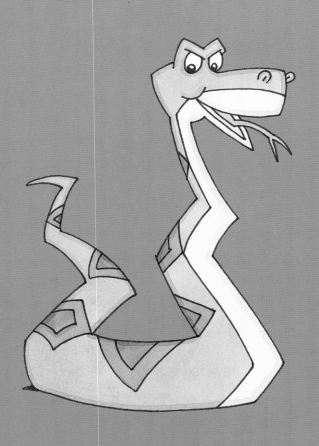

the snake

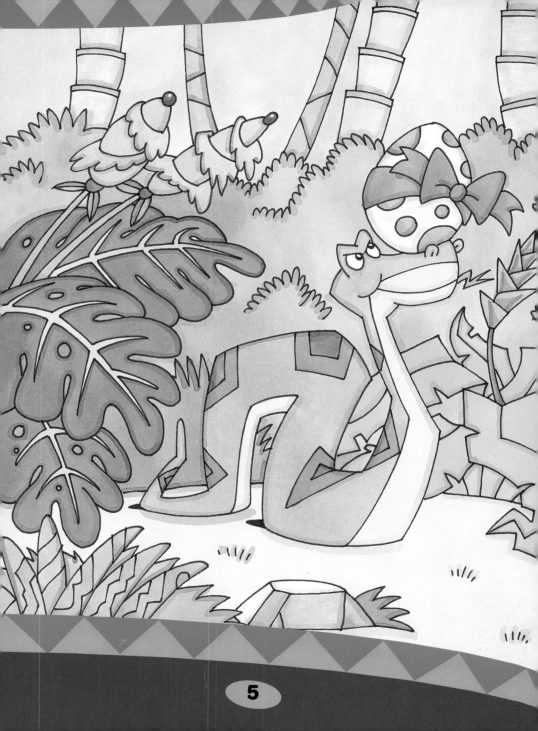

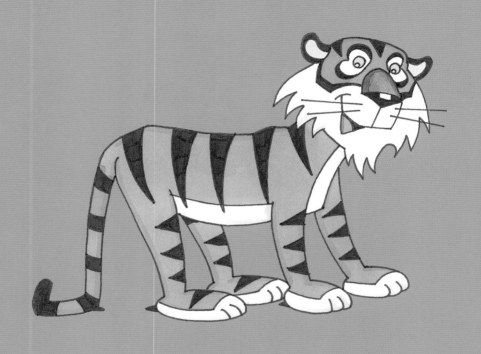

the tiger

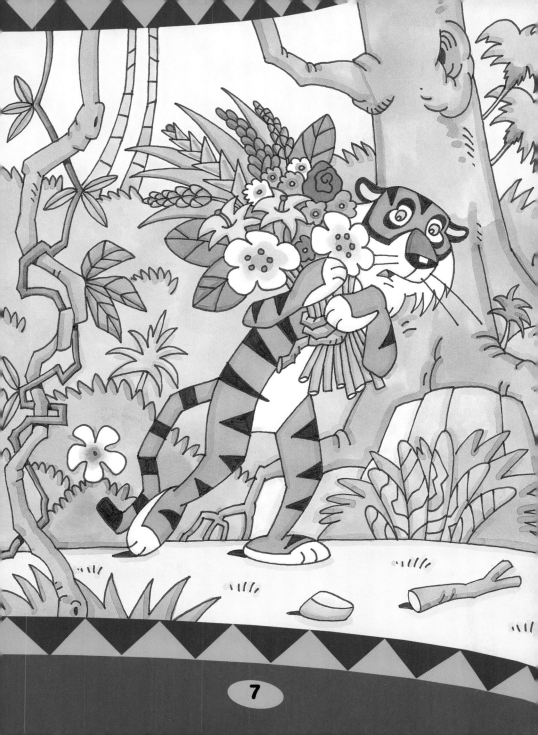

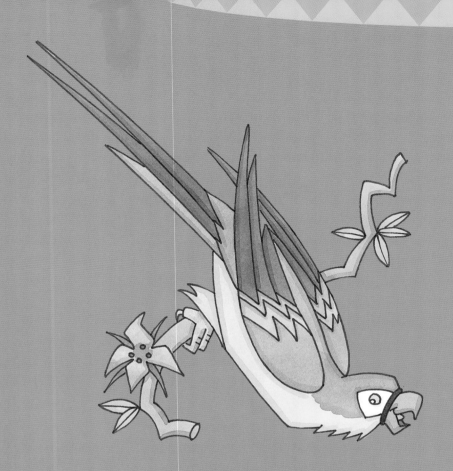

the bird

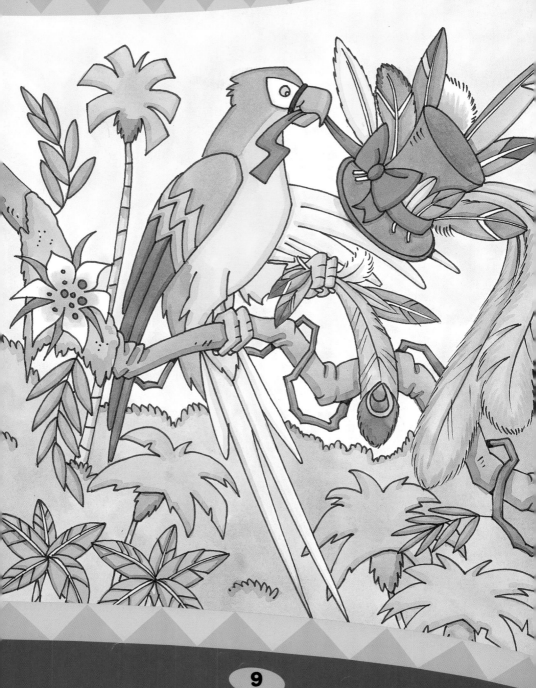

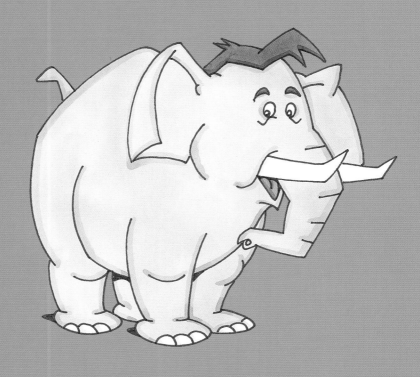

the elephant

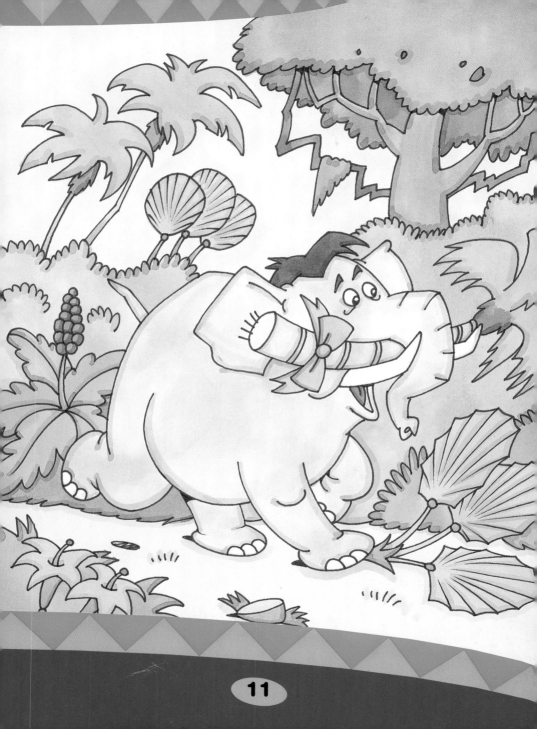

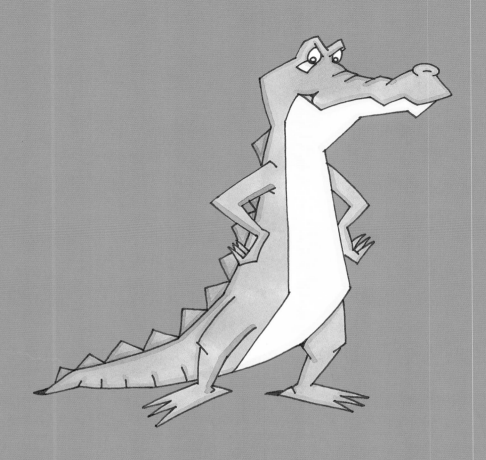

the crocodile

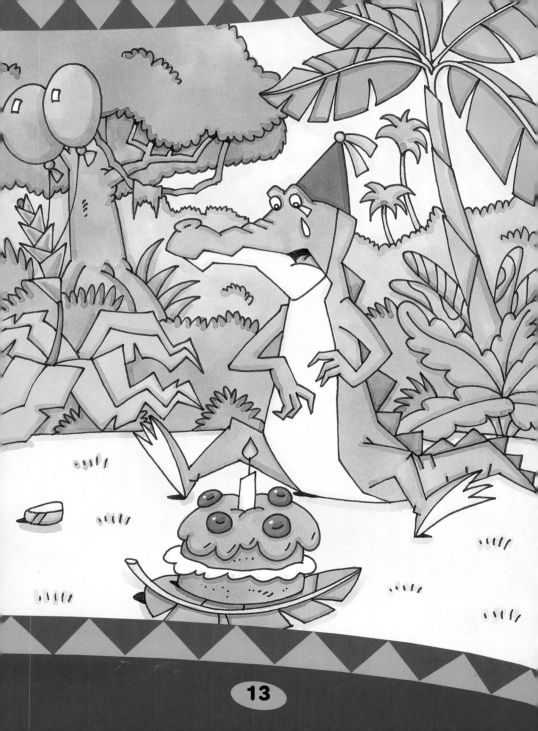

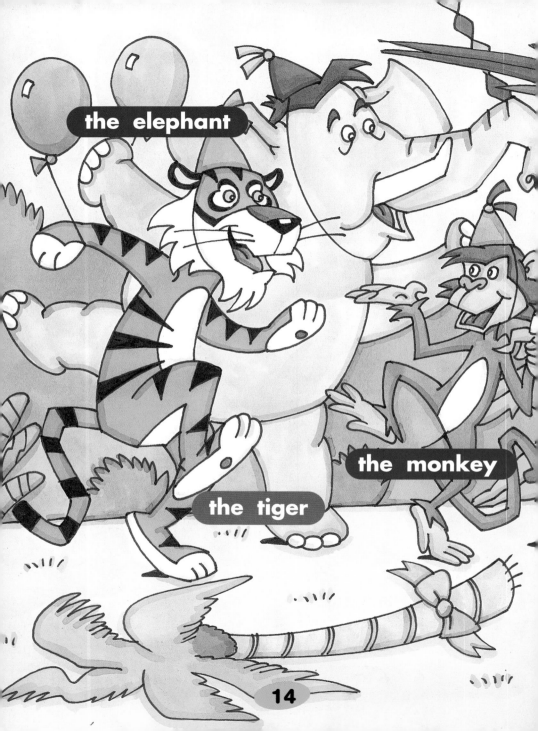

the elephant

the monkey

the tiger

14

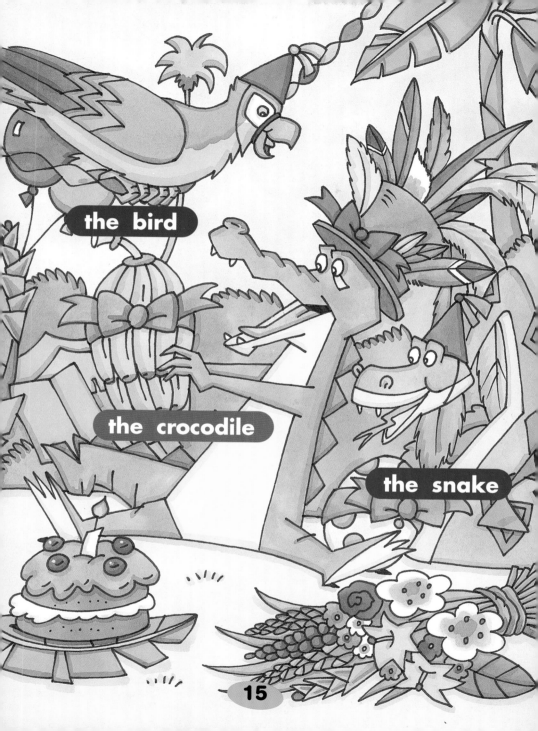

the bird

the crocodile

the snake

15

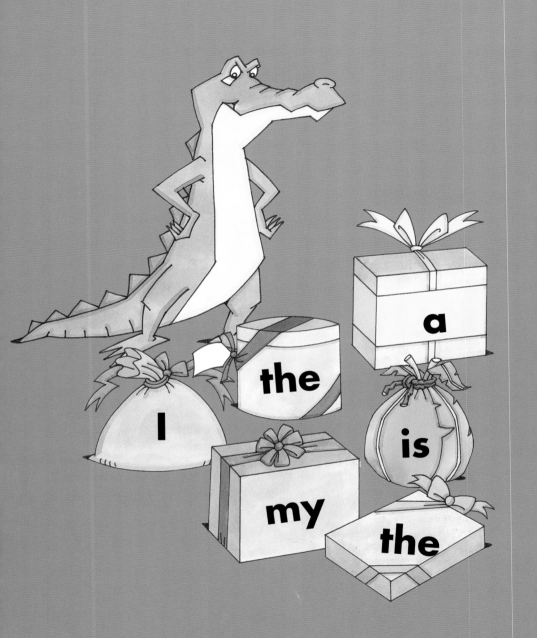